This book belongs to:

....

....

....

Retold by Gaby Goldsack
Illustrated by Emma Lake (Advocate)
Designed by Jester Designs

Language consultant: Betty Root

ISBN 1-84461-140-X

Marks and Spencer p.l.c.
PO Box 3339, Chester CH99 9QS
www.marksandspencer.com

The Emperor's New Clothes

Helping Your Child to Read

Learning to read is an exciting challenge for most children. From a very early age, sharing story books with children, talking about the pictures and guessing what might happen next are all very important parts of the reading experience.

Sharing reading

Set aside a regular quiet time to share reading with younger children, or to be on hand to encourage older children as they develop into independent readers.

First Readers are intended to encourage and support the early stages of learning to read. They present well-loved tales that children will happily listen to again and again. Familiarity helps children to identify some of the words and phrases.

When you feel your child is ready to move on a little, encourage them to join in so that you read the story aloud together. Always pause to talk about the pictures. The easy-to-read speech bubbles in **First Readers** provide an excellent 'joining-in' activity. The bright, clear illustrations and matching text will help children to understand the story.

Building confidence

In time, children will want to read *to* you. When this happens, be patient and give continual praise. They may not read all the words correctly, but children's substitutions are often very good guesses.

The repetition in each book is particularly helpful for building confidence. If your child cannot read a particular word, go back to the beginning of the sentence and read it together so the meaning is not lost. Most importantly, do not continue if your child is tired or simply in need of a change.

Reading aloud

The next step is to ask your child to read aloud to you. This does require patience and perseverance. Remember to give lots of encouragement and praise.

Together with other simple stories, **First Readers** will ensure that children will find reading an enjoyable and rewarding experience.

Once upon a time there was an Emperor who loved clothes. He spent all his money on new clothes. He would change five or six times a day.

One day, two clever thieves came to see
the Emperor. They told the Emperor
that they were weavers.

"We can weave beautiful cloth,"
said one thief.

"And it is magic," said the other.
"Only clever people can see the cloth.
Stupid people see nothing."

"Make me a suit from this magic cloth," said the Emperor. "Then I will be able to tell who is clever and who is stupid."

"We will need lots of gold thread," said the first thief.

So the Emperor gave them lots of gold thread.

13

The thieves put the gold thread into their bags. Then they pretended to weave the cloth but they did not use the gold thread.

Really they were doing nothing at all.

The next day, the Emperor sent his
Prime Minister to see the cloth.

The Prime Minister looked and looked.
He could not see anything.

"I must be stupid," he thought.
"The Emperor must not find out."

He told the Emperor that it was the
best cloth he had ever seen.

The next day, the two thieves went to see the Emperor.

"We need more gold thread to make your suit," said the first thief.
"You shall have all the thread you need," said the Emperor.

The two thieves pretended to make the cloth into a suit.

The Emperor went to see the suit.
He looked and looked.
He could not see anything.

"I must be stupid," he thought. "No one must find out."

"It is beautiful!" he cried.

The Emperor was very pleased.

He spoke to the Prime Minister.

"We must have a parade. Everyone

will be able to see my new suit."

The two thieves pretended to work all day and all night.

At last the suit was ready.

The Emperor came to try on his new suit.

"It will feel lovely. It will feel as if you are wearing nothing," said the first thief.

They pretended to dress the Emperor in his new suit.

The Emperor and his Prime Minister looked and looked, but they could not see anything.

The Emperor led the parade in his new suit. Everyone looked and looked, but they could not see the new suit.

Then one little girl started to laugh. "The Emperor has no clothes on," she cried.

And soon everyone, even the Emperor, saw that she was right.

"Oh no!" said the Emperor. "I have been very stupid."

And the thieves were never seen again.

I have been very stupid.

Read and Say

How many of these words can you say?
The pictures will help you. Look back in
your book and see if you can find the
words in the story.

Emperor

thieves

gold thread

clothes

money

Prime Minister

little girl

parade

Titles in this series,
subject to availability:

Beauty and the Beast
Chicken-Licken
Cinderella
The Elves and the Shoemaker
The Emperor's New Clothes
The Enormous Turnip
The Gingerbread Man
Goldilocks and the Three Bears
Hansel and Gretel
Jack and the Beanstalk
Joseph's Coat of Many Colours
and Other Bible Stories
Little Red Riding Hood
Noah's Ark and Other Bible Stories
Rapunzel
Rumpelstiltskin
Sleeping Beauty
Snow White and the Seven Dwarfs
The Three Billy Goats Gruff
The Three Little Pigs
The Ugly Duckling